WICKED INK CHRONICLES

FIRST *ink*

NEW YORK TIMES BESTSELLING AUTHOR

LAURA WRIGHT

Cover Designer: Sweet 'n Spicy Designs by Jaycee DeLorenzo

Editor: JuliaEdits

Interior Designer: Jovana Shirley, Unforeseen Editing, www.unforeseenediting.com

ISBN-13: 978-0-9860641-8-0

Addison

"Oh my god," Lisa says, staring at the billboard covering one massive wall of the convention center. "He is the hottest thing that ever walked the earth. You should've warned me, Addy."

I don't say a thing. Just tear my gaze from the black and white photograph on the billboard and head for the virtual mosh pit of bodies stretching out in front of us. My heart is slamming furiously against my ribs as I push up on my tiptoes and try to see over the crowd, see the live version of what Lisa and I have been staring at for a good five minutes. But it's impossible. Inked bodies with stilettos and mohawks block my view of the man—the attraction—in the center. As I hear the buzzing sound of a tattoo needle at work, I suddenly wish I had worn heels and a color other than beige.

"There must be five hundred people here," Lisa says, awe threading her voice. "Just to watch him work. Is he famous or something?"

"Very," I say as we walk around the circle of spectators, trying to find a way in.

Lisa is much more appropriately dressed than I am for a tattoo convention, in a pink miniskirt and tight black t-shirt that shows off her small but firm rack. More than a few guys have noticed her already, and maybe even a girl or two—something I know she loves probably more than she should. The girl is a terrible flirt, and really stands out with her long mane of nearly white blond hair and crystal blue eyes.

"Does he tattoo celebrities and rockers and models and people like that?" she asks, searching the crowd for an opening.

"That's what I hear," I say.

I'm clearly offering as little information as possible on what I know about Rush's life. And the frown Lisa keeps throwing my way lets me know it's starting to piss her off. A fact I can live with as I'm really not up for telling her how closely I follow him.

"This is bullshit." She grabs my hand. "We're going to cut."

"Wait, Lis." I don't want to cause a scene. Really don't want Rush to see me yet. Not when he can walk in the opposite direction.

Lisa turns those pale blue eyes on me. The ones that say, 'Hey, girlie, I just drove six hours from

L.A. to be here with you. We both know why. And I'm not hanging in the back when the action is up front.'

This, of course, is all in my mind. What she actually says is, "This is it, Addy. You've been working this problem for five years now. Do you want to see him or not?"

Just the thought of going face to face with Rush again makes me nauseated as hell. I fist my shaking hands and press them to my sides.

"I know this can't be easy," Lisa continues. "But I'm with you a hundred percent, okay?"

"Okay," I manage to get out before another wave of nausea hits me.

"We have a plan," she says.

"Absolutely."

"Tell me the plan, Addison."

Lisa is my best friend, and the one person on earth who has my back. And it's odd because we're complete opposites. We met the second week of classes our freshman year at UC Santa Barbara, and instantly clicked. Same English major, same desire to live off campus. This good girl from a wealthy family who wanted to be bad, and me, a girl who grew up with nothing, and was tossed around from place to place, but always dreamed of a different life. A stable life. A real life.

"The plan is," I say, wetting my lips because they've gone so dry they hurt. "We go up to him after the demonstration. You chat up his handler, while I try and get him alone."

She cocks her head to the side. "Did the plan sound better in the car?"

"Shut up!" I go off, half laughing.

She grins. “Come on.”

We try to move closer, deeper into the crowd, but before we make it to the third tier a couple of girls shoulder us back. They glare at us, copping some major attitude, thinking we’re trying take their spot. Which we kind of are, so we back off again. I’m not nearly as badass as I used to be. Back in the day I probably would’ve gotten in their faces, shared some words.

Further down, we spot a fissure in the throng and hurry toward it. Lisa heads in first, her body language all determined now, ready to take on any chick even if she has a legitimate reason to be pissed at us.

“You can’t get close to him without a special pass,” I hear a girl say to her friend as we snake through. “But they say it’s only for taking a picture with him.”

“Are you serious?” the other girl says. “He’s not doing any more ink today?”

“Just this one piece. He normally doesn’t go to conventions.”

“Fuck,” the girl said on a groan. “I’ve been on his waiting list for six months. I thought this would be my chance.”

“Well, if you get to take a picture with him maybe you can convince him to get you in sooner.”

The woman pressed her breasts together and grinned. “I do have two very powerful methods of persuasion.”

Lisa leans in and whispers in my ear. “First of all, gross. Second, we need to get you a picture with him.”

I shake my head. A picture is the last thing I want from Rush. I have plenty. Of him. Of us. What I want—what I need—is to be able to get a few minutes alone with him. To apologize for what I did five years ago. The concept sounded so simple, but so far he's rejected my every attempt. Calls, letters, even trying to get on the waiting list at his tattoo shop, Wicked Ink. He wants nothing to do with me. And I don't blame him.

It was a complete fluke that someone at school was talking about the Las Vegas tattoo convention, and getting some ink done before graduation in six weeks. I didn't think Rush would be there. He seems to never work outside his shop. But when I heard he would be, I packed up the car, pretended I didn't have finals bearing down on me and convinced Lisa to ride shotgun.

There's a sudden shift in the crowd, and Lisa and I bump into each other. Everyone seems to be moving forward like an ocean wave. Then I see a woman being helped up onto a chair. She's young, early twenties like me, really pretty, very tatted up and dressed like a 1950's pin-up girl. Her dark eyes scan the crowd and she brings a microphone to her cherry-red lips.

"Okay, Assholes," she says in the sweetest of tones, her voice booming over the din of hard-driving music and buzzing needles. "He says he'll take one more."

Like a clap of thunder, the crowd goes nuts. My heart flies into my throat with the intensity. Hands shoot into the air, tickets clasped in their fingers, fluttering like a mass of yellow butterflies.

The woman grins wickedly, and her diamond nose piercing flashes in the lights. She's got some serious charisma. Like the kind that not only brings guys to their knees, but makes them want to crawl around on the floor for a while.

"But," she says real drawn out-like. "He wants a virgin."

The disappointment is instant. As I try to figure out what the girl is talking about, all around me, both men and women—but frankly, a lot more women—toss around the stink face and shake their heads.

"So…" Ms. Pin-Up says. "Any ink virgins here today?"

Three hands go up, and to my utter shock and horror, one of them is Lisa's. And though I'm relieved we're all talking about virginal *tattoos* here, my eyes cut to her instantly. “What are you doing?”

“I don’t know,” she laughs, her face pink and excited.

“Put your hand down,” I hiss. “Before they—”

“You!” Ms. Pin-Up calls out.

Before I even turn back, I know the girl is pointing at Lisa. Eyes wide, my crazy-assed best friend bites her lip, then grabs my hand. “Come on.”

“Don’t do this,” I said, my old nemesis nausea creeping back to stake claim to my stomach.

“Too late, Addy.” She sounds completely giddy, like her brain has turned into Skittles. “Besides, here’s your way in.”

“This wasn’t the plan,” I argue.

“Fuck the plan, Addy. Sometimes you just have to jump.”

I'm about to tell her that getting in the car and driving to Vegas, not telling anyone, no hotel room, is jumping, but Ms. Pin-Up is staring at us expectantly. Along with about a hundred other people.

"Come on up here, sweetheart," she calls, motioning for Lisa to step forward.

"Oh my god, oh my god," Lisa squeals softly, pulling me with her, squeezing my hand so hard I flinch.

This time, instead of blocking our way, the crowd parts, Red Sea-style, and in seconds we're in the front of the pack. Lisa drops my hand and follows the woman, leaving me there in my conservative beige skirt and pale blue top to stare at the guy I haven't seen in five years. The guy who has never once left my thoughts, no matter how hard I've tried to push him out.

My stomach rolls so painfully I feel like I might pass out. Back in high school, Rush Merrick was a shockingly good-looking kid. Tall, lean, badass attitude. Sexy brown hair, eyes so green they looked like leaves in the sun. But now he's something else. And frankly, the photograph on the wall behind me, the one Lisa had drooled over, doesn't do him justice. He's utterly and totally breath-stealing. And I get the crowd now. I get the women.

As he speaks to Ms. Pin-Up, my eyes move over him, up and down. He's even taller now, still lean, but with cords and waves of muscle that make my hands twitch involuntarily. I fist them again, inviting carpal tunnel, trying to force away the impulse to touch him. But instead my mouth starts to water.

He's wearing really simple clothes, but on him they're sexy as shit. A black tank top that shows off his ripped muscles and sleeves of vibrant tattoos, jeans that hang on his lean hips, black combat boots. And as I scale his hotness one more time it occurs to me that though he still has a boy's wicked grin, he's a man everywhere else.

Lisa steps forward, her face as pink as her miniskirt. I've never seen her so timid and girlie, and I kind of want to slap her. 'What about the fucking plan?' I want to yell. Then I hear the voice that used to make my toes curl—and my heart beat twice as fast—rise above the din.

"You my virgin skin?" he asks her, his eyes doing a sexy half-lidded thing that I remember was usually followed up by a bone-melting kiss.

I roll my eyes at my resurrected eleventh grade self.

"I may have virgin skin," Lisa tells him, her voice shaking slightly. "But that's the only virgin thing on me."

He laughs, a low rumble in his chest. And my breath is stuck inside my lungs—possibly permanently.

Lisa grins really wide. "In fact, I think I might be pregnant."

My mouth falls open, and that hostage breath is released. Okay, slapping isn't going to cut it. Lisa is clearly having a Crazy Town moment that may require pills.

"Sorry, doll," Rush says, glancing over at Ms. Pin-Up like maybe they should start screening the volunteer flesh. "We don't ink anyone who might be knocked up."

The crowd boos en masse, and in that moment I'm trying to figure out a way to get Lisa and sprint for the back of the convention center.

"Looks like we need another virgin," Ms. Pin-Up calls. "And if you're a true virgin, even better. No one with a bun in the oven, people, okay?"

"Wait," Lisa calls out. "My friend's a virgin. Hey, Addison, come here!"

Heat slams into my body and I can't feel my limbs. Heads turn to me, eyes narrowed, and there's nothing I want more than to get the hell out of here and plan Lisa's very ugly, very painful demise.

What about the fucking plan, whore?

But then Rush turns, and his eyes lock to mine, and I'm rooted to the floor. Even if I wanted to move, I don't think I could. It's been so long, and he's so beautiful. His lips look dark and full, surrounded by a night or two's worth of stubble. And his hair is longer than I've ever seen it, the dark brown edges licking his hard jawline. But it's his eyes—always been his eyes—that make my insides tremble. They're so green and so filled with hostility as he stares at me.

He wants me nowhere near him.

Lisa's on her way over, her expression wary. "Okay, okay," she says when she reaches me. "I know you hate me right now, but that plan wouldn't have worked. I'll be right here. Watching you."

"Pregnant?" I grind out.

She shrugs. "It's not entirely out of the realm of possibility."

"You're going to totally suck as a mother," I say halfheartedly as my feet are released from the invisible concrete and I walk past her, toward the guy I used to want more than I wanted a real family.

He watches my every step, his eyes moving down my body, taking in my clothes, my shoes. I know exactly what he sees and what he's thinking. 'What the hell happened to you? Where's your boyfriend, Ken Doll? Why the fuck can't you take a hint and leave me alone?'

And then we're face to face. I'm standing in front of him, and he smells so good and looks so fierce, and I think I might be dizzy because the last time it was like this, I betrayed and humiliated him in front of an entire room full of people. My best friend. My only friend.

Mismatched eyes that have haunted the shit out of me for too many years to count—too many years to not call myself a gigantic pussy—stare up at me. They're liquid and fearful, and they make me want to grab her and kiss her so hard she starts crying and runs away. Yeah, I want to make *her* run away this time. But I can't. I won't. I have an audience, and they've come to see a show.

I let my eyes do the work, move down her body, take in that crazy, garden party-looking shit she's wearing. I have no idea what she's been up to since high school, never wanted to know, because I might've gone after her. And there was no way in hell I was jumping on board that train again.

She fucking murdered my heart. It still beats, but not nearly as strong.

"What's your name again?" I ask, then watch impassively as hurt flickers in her eyes.

"Addison," she says.

Shit, her voice is like a fucking vise to my cock. My eyes narrow on her. "You pregnant, Addison?"

She looks around, at everyone who's waiting, listening, then comes back to me, shakes her head. "No."

The lights in the center are killer bright, and they make her brown hair shimmer. I notice that it's gotten longer and lighter. Damn if I don't remember what it feels like all tangled up in my fingers.

"Any other reason why I shouldn't touch you today?" I ask.

She swallows, and I watch the movement in her throat so closely like it's the best goddamn movie I've ever seen.

"No," she says.

"Then let's get started."

I start to back up, but she reaches out and grabs my wrist. "Wait."

My skin burns where she's holding it. But even so, I don't pull away. My eyes lift and I utter, "What's up?"

"We didn't talk about what I wanted."

"No. We didn't." I swear to fucking god it's like the two of us are the only ones in the joint now. I know there's a crowd. I know Jane's watching me from her perch on the chair, probably wondering what the hell's my problem. But shit, I don't hear anything but Addison's voice, and I'm not seeing anything but her eyes, one blue, one green. The green one is almost the exact same color as mine. It'd been our thing. That eye of hers would only look at me. It belonged to me.

She belonged to me.

"Maybe something really small?" she says, her thin fingers still wrapped around my wrist. "A butterfly or a heart."

My mouth curves into a grin. "You didn't know?"

"Know what?" she asks.

"The skin doesn't get to choose the ink. Not here. I decide what I want on you."

Panic glitters in her eyes, and I can't help but get off on it.

"You really asking me to draw a heart on you, Addison?" I say.

Her teeth scrape against her top lip, and after a moment she releases me. She shakes her head. “Do what you want, Rush.”

It’s the first time she’s used my name, and every goddamn memory of her whispering it, calling it out, moaning it in my ear, comes at me like a fucking firing squad.

I lift an eyebrow at her. “Wherever I want?”

She nods.

My body is stoked up and I know I’d better cool down if I’m going to be holding a needle to her skin.

I lean in and whisper, “You trust me, Addison?”

She shivers instantly. “Trust has nothing to do with this. Nothing to do with why I’m here.”

"Yeah, I know," I tell her. Because I do. The reason was in every email I never opened, every letter I sent back unread, every phone call I ignored. "You want something from me I'll never give you."

Her eyes hold me captive. They always did.

"You have to," she says, her voice reed-thin.

I shake my head. Around us the crowd is getting restless. I don't give a shit about them, and I know I should.

"You have to, Rush," she says again, more impassioned this time. "I can't…" She stops, looks away.

I hate that I care. I fucking hate it. And yet I ask, "You can't what?"

It was her turn to shake her head. "Nothing. I'm ready. For you, for whatever you choose." She lifts her chin. "For my first ink."

The crowd explodes into hoots and catcalls. They've waited long enough. Maybe I have, too. Getting her skin under me again. Not for pleasure, but for pain.

I back up and motion to my chair. "Fine. Take off your shirt and lie down."

Addison

I stare at him, watch him as he goes over to Ms. Pin-Up and whispers something in her ear. I have no idea what he's saying, but when he's done she glances up and gives me a strange look. Kind of like I just stepped out of a toilet, and she doesn't know whether to be disgusted by me or pity me. I wonder if she's his girlfriend. This beautiful, vibrant, tatted-up sex kitten. *A girlfriend.* It's a thought I hadn't entertained in years, if ever. But it's a thought that makes me unbearably sad.

Heading over to his station, Rush thrusts his hands inside a pair of thin, black latex gloves, then lifts an eyebrow at me. "Are we doing this?"

"Yes," I tell him, praying to god I don't lose my nerve. Lisa was right. This could be the way to talk with him. Even if it is in front of hundreds of people.

Taking in my moment's hesitation, his eyes move down my body. "You're still wearing that shirt, and your ass is nowhere near my table."

Wait, I think, with a sudden drop of my heart into my shoes. *He was serious about that?* "Do you really need my top off? Or is this just a way to humiliate me?"

"Why would that humiliate you, Addison? If I remember things right you have one extraordinarily beautiful body." He shrugged. "Course in that blue pillowcase you're wearing it's hard to tell."

My face goes hot, and his eyes flash with amusement like he's really enjoying seeing me squirm.

"Take it off already," some guy yells from the crowd.

I look around and catch Lisa's gaze. From her spot in the front row, she looks guilty and worried, and she mouths the words, "Do you want to go?" followed by a grimace.

I quickly shake my head.

"No one's here to see your tits, honey," the same guy calls out. "Get someone else, Rush. This bitch is off."

Rush walks past me without a word. His face is tight, so's his body, but it's his eyes that really freak me out. They're dark and deadly, and ice-cold. He dips into the crowd. I don't know how he knows where the guy is, but he does.

"Get the fuck out of here, dude," he says with absolute calm.

The guy sniffs. He's probably somewhere in his mid-thirties, and nearly the same height as Rush, but thicker around the middle. "I just want to watch, man. What's the big deal? Shit."

"Big deal is you don't talk to a lady like that. It's not cool, and it's not tolerated."

"Fuck you," the guy says, then gives Rush a shove.

Rush sends his fist into the guy's gut, then grabs him by the back of the head and slams his knee into the man's stunned face.

"I really hate these conventions," I hear Rush say.

As I watch dumbfounded, the guy goes down on his knees and remains there, intermittently wheezing and moaning. As the crowd falls quiet, Rush gestures to someone near the back, and in seconds two guys dressed in black haul Mr. Charming away.

Eyes as cool as twin emeralds, Rush heads back my way, pulling off his gloves. The knuckles on his right hand are bleeding. "Keep your bra on, baby. No one'll see a thing."

I turn, my eyes following him, my heart pounding fast and sick. He's such a frighteningly, deliciously volatile creature, and I just want to know what it feels like to be taken over by him again.

As he washes up in the sink, I unbutton my shirt. My fingers shake as I work off each small, silver circle like it's a puzzle piece. My brain isn't working right. It wants to work out other answers to other puzzles like, why did he do that? Why did he challenge that guy? Knock him down when he hates me so much?

Rush slips on a clean pair of gloves, then looks up, locks eyes with me. He motions for me to come to him. My skin instantly reacts to the command by going hot and tight. I walk over, shrug out of my shirt and place it on the back of an empty chair. Cool air moves over my hot skin, but it's Rush's gaze moving over my skin that truly brings out the goose bumps. It's hungry and dark, and I can't help but get a little thrill that I still affect him in some way.

"Lie down," he says, his tone as tight as his jaw.

I climb onto the table and stretch out, rest my cheek on my hands so I can watch him. Rush pushes his black swivel stool close to my shoulder blades and checks his materials all set out on a metal table by Ms. Pin-Up. Then he looks down at me.

"You okay?" he asks.

I take a deep breath and wonder again why I'm doing this. This—as in, letting him permanently ink my skin with a design of his own choosing. Is it just to get him to talk to me? Listen to me? Or is there more? Do I want him to touch me? Be forced to touch me?

"I don't like pain," I say.

His eyes flash as he reaches across my back to unhook my bra. "No one does, baby. No one does."

As I try not to obsess over his words and their obvious meaning, I watch him pick up a razor from the table and lean over me. I feel his hard stomach press against my arm as he runs the thing over my upper back a few times. Next, I feel a cool, wet cloth dragging gently across my skin. Then what feels like paper, about the size of an orange, pressing firmly into the area, then lifting away.

He reappears in my eyeline and asks, “Ready?”

My mouth is so damn dry I just nod, then brace myself.

As the needle touches my skin, and Rush draws the first line of whatever image he’s chosen, I close my eyes and breathe. It doesn’t hurt nearly as bad as I thought it would, but I know it’s going to be a long process and I have to prepare myself for what’s coming.

Over the next ten minutes, I let the sound of the machine lull me into a strange sense of calm. As I continue to rest my cheek on my hands, I vacillate between eyes closed and eyes open, and trying to figure out what he's drawing by the movements of the needle. But so far, I've got nothing.

From what I can see, Rush is concentrating really hard, his eyes pinned to my skin, his face tight with tension. It's incredibly hot, and I wish I had a better view.

"Rush," I say in a quiet voice, not wanting to jolt him from his focus. "Can I talk while you work?"

"Depends on what you have to say."

"Just…thanks."

His nostrils flare, but his hand is shockingly steady. "You can thank me after you see it."

"No," I correct him. "I mean for the asshole in the crowd."

The bite of the needle is gone momentarily. And I realize he's lifted it off my skin. His eyes flicker to mine. "It's nothing."

Then he returns to his work. I settle in to watching him again, completely unaware of the crowd, of Lisa, of everyone but him. It was always like that back when we were together. He was addictive. Like sugar. Like horror movies. Sometimes after we'd have sex I'd just lie there and stare at him, tell myself over and over that he was mine. That this gorgeous, talented boy belonged to me, wanted me, loved me. I saw us together, sharing an apartment as we went to college.

And then I got moved from my aunt's house into a foster home, and then another foster home, and then a group home, and eventually everything I wanted and hoped for and believed in got crushed. Not by anyone I knew. God, that would've been so much easier to forgive. But by me.

"Is it starting to hurt?" Rush asks me, lifting the needle again, cocking his head to the side, his eyes finding mine. "You're tensing up."

"No," I assure him. "Just thinking."

He doesn't ask. Instead his eyes return to my back. When the needle makes contact again, my mind tries to follow the lines it's making. I sense a diamond shape, but I can't figure it out.

"Are you going to tell me what you're tattooing on me now?" I ask.

"You'll see for yourself when it's done."

"How about a hint? Like if it's something gross or pornographic or just really, really mean."

I see the corners of his mouth twitch. God, he's so sexy. Forget Ms. Pin-Up. He probably has a hundred girlfriends. All on speed dial. All waiting with bated breath for him to call.

I know I would be.

"It's not a portrait of me flipping you off or anything," he says.

"Okay, good." I make a face. "That's a relief."

His eyes darken. "Don't get cute with me, okay? You've wanted to get under my needle for what…two years now?"

I sober a little at his combative mood. "I think it's going on three. Didn't realize your wait list was that long."

"It's not." Once again, he lifts the needle off my skin, gives me a look so dead sexy my breasts tingle against the table.

"You know, I never wanted a tattoo," I say.

"Yeah, I know. That's why you never got an appointment."

I release a breath. "I just wanted a chance to talk to you."

"Well, you got it. Or your girlfriend did. Either way, I'm here, you're here. Go."

"Okay." I bite my lip. It felt so easy a second ago. Now my brain doesn't want to cooperate. "It's just…there's a lot of people here…"

"And?"

"And I know it's kind of loud in here, but are you cool with someone, I don't know, in the front row maybe, hearing how I feel about you? How what I did five years ago is tearing me up? How every time someone touches me or kisses me I wish it was you?"

The sound of the tattoo machine dies, and Rush's eyes cut to mine. They're like twin daggers, and I can't tell if he's turned on or pissed off. Either way, my heart leaps hardcore into my throat. He looks up, gestures—no doubt to Ms. Pin-Up—and in seconds, I'm cleaned off and something warm is rubbed into my back. His jaw tight, Rush places a cloth over my tattoo and tapes around it, then re-clasps my bra.

"You can sit up now and put on your shirt," he tells me coolly, ripping off his gloves.

I'm confused. Not by his tone—that I was expecting—but by the quick work. I always assumed tats took a few hours. "That's it?"

"For now," he says.

For now? As in, there's more? "What the hell, Rush?"

He's tossing his gloves in the trash, but as soon as they hit the rim, he rounds on me and places a hand on either side of my hip, locking me into his vibrantly tattooed airspace. The breath leaves my body as my gaze travels over his collarbone, which sports a skull interwoven with the letters of his last name. As I sit there in my boring bra and my even more boring skirt, his face closes in on mine, and I swear if I lean forward an inch I can press my lips to his. *Does he taste the same?* I wonder. *Feel the same*?

"You want to talk to me," he says, his warm breath moving over my skin, making me shiver. "You want to finish this tat? We'll do it my way."

His way. Oh, god, I used to love doing things his way. I contemplate sticking my tongue out and lapping at the air, seeing if I can taste him that way.

"Be at my shop at eleven tonight," he says. "Alone."

I nod dumbly and mumble a raspy, "Okay."

But instead of leaning closer, giving me what I think he knows I want, he releases me, pushes away. I instantly want him back.

Sound familiar, Addison?

My shirt is shoved into my hands by Ms. Pin-Up, and I stand up and get busy putting it on, buttoning it up. My heart is still knocking against my ribs and my insides feel almost as liquid as certain parts of my outsides. I don't care about the dissolving crowd or how Lisa's on her way over to me with a look of utter horror. All I care about is tonight, and seeing him again. Explaining things, asking for forgiveness.

Getting his hands on me again.

"And Addison," he calls.

I turn so easily, almost involuntarily, toward the sound of his voice, like it controls me now.

He slips on a black knit cap, his eyes flashing emerald fire my way. "Don't look at it. If you take off the bandage, I'll know."

I'm home. Outside of Vegas, near the Red Rocks where I belong, where I can breathe. Inside my shop, Wicked Ink, the buzz of three tattoo machines rends the air. Vincent, Jane and I are all working on our final clients. Well, V and Janie are anyway. I got one last piece coming in at eleven.

"You're quiet tonight, man."

"Just focusing, brother," I say, adjusting my hand pressure. This cover-up on my old friend, Cory, is a monster—a bullshit tribal with heavy black ink and some scarring—and I want to make sure I get it right before he heads back to L.A. and whatever movie he's making.

"You had that convention today, right?" he asks me.

I pull my needle back and dilute the color in some water. "Never doing one of those again. Not my scene."

"Even with all the hot chicks?"

I grin at him. "Even then."

He sighs, drops his head back against the chair. "Chicks with tattoos rock my world. And if they have a few piercings in some very private places, even better."

I shake my head. The guy pretends to be such a cupcake on the red carpet. "Sounds like you need to hit the convention next time."

As he laughs, Vincent sticks his head in the room. The guy's black hair has just been recently skull-shaved. Between that, his black eyes and the nearly full body art, he looks like one of the death rockers Jane loves to ink. Except for the face. Boy's got a fucking Hollywood face.

"Hey, Rush, man," he says. "There's someone here for you, and she's not on the books."

I feel the announcement of her presence in my gut. It sits there and grinds away, pain and pleasure all at the same time. Sure, I'd given her Wicked's address, and her ink wasn't close to being done, but I'd seriously wondered if she'd show. Wondered if she'd run again.

Like a pussy, I'd even thought about sending a car for her. Or picking her up on my bike. But my pride found its way back to my balls.

I glance up at Vincent again. "Tell her to have a seat."

“Sure thing.” He grins real wide at me, his eyebrows going up and down.

“What are you doing, idiot?”

“Or I could take her. You know,” he shrugs. “I have a softer touch than you do with the iron.”

“Yeah, but women don’t want a softer touch,” I say. “Especially when you’re using your iron.”

Cory laughs, and I grin. We’re all such fucking infants sometimes. Thank god we have Janie in the shop. That cool-as-ice pin-up balances us all out. And by ‘balances’ I mean she tells us we’re complete knuckleheads, and that if we don’t grow the hell up, she’s outta there.

And that ain’t happening. We can’t do without our Janie. Girl’s the shit. Eight month waiting list tells the truth of it: every rocker, rapper and reggae artist on the West Coast wants a tattoo from her.

Plus, she's cool. She'd really helped me out today, with the asshats at the convention, and with Addison. No judgment.

"You suddenly have time on your hands?" I say to V. "I thought you were booked all day."

"I was. Am." He drops his chin, gives me the innocent look. "I'm done for the night. I could help you out."

And I give him a fuck off grin. "I got it, V. Thanks for having my back though."

"Anytime, man." He pushes away from the door. "And by anytime I mean when a girl's as smoking hot as this one."

My gut twists up again like a fucking piece of licorice. Something inside of me doesn't like hearing another guy talk about Addison that way. Granted, it's true. She is smoking hot. But the caveman inside me wants to drag Vincent out back behind the dumpsters and kick the crap out of his Hollywood ass just for noticing.

"Shit," I hiss under my breath, rubbing some goo into Cory's finished piece before wrapping it up. I'm not going here again. Not letting myself go here again. Finish Addison's tat, let her say her piece, get her off my ass and back where she belongs.

"Meet someone at the convention, brother?" Cory asks me as he unfolds from the chair.

"Just an old friend," I tell him.

"Doesn't sound old," he says as I walk him out the door.

First thing we both see is Addison in the waiting area. She's sitting on the black leather couch, the brick wall at her back, flipping through my book. It's nuts how hard it makes me just watching her look at my artwork. She's changed her clothes. No more garden party downstairs, no more pillowcase up top. Instead she has on a white wifebeater tank and a pair of pretty tight-fitting faded jeans. She looks casual and sexy, and I can see why Vincent was ready to give up his Saturday night for a few hours of working on her skin.

She looks up from the book then, and her eyes find mine and lock into place. They're worried, they're hungry, and they make me deliriously happy by not even flickering in Cory's direction. The dude is a movie star, for chrissakes.

"Doesn't sound old," Cory says again, this time under his breath as he shakes my hand. "And definitely doesn't look like a friend."

"Nice to see you again, man." I knock my chin at the glass door leading to the parking lot. "Good luck on the film."

Cory gets the hint loud and clear, and with a wry grin, and a quick look at Addison, he takes a hike.

Once we're alone in the waiting room, aka the rec room, I give her a nod. "Hey there."

"Sorry I'm early." She shrugs, her sexy, tanned shoulders lifting and lowering. "I'm happy to hang out for a while if you're not ready."

"I'm ready," I say too damn quickly. "Come on in."

She follows me into my den. When I built this place, I wanted to make sure there were private rooms as well as open ones, and it was a good thing too, because several of our more famous clients really appreciate it.

As she takes in the space, I close the door and lock it without thinking. Or, fuck me, maybe I am thinking. Maybe I'm thinking that I don't want V or Janie interrupting us.

"This is so you."

Her words, and the familiar warmth she coats them in, bring my head around. She's checking out my home away from home, her back to me, offering up one hella spectacular view of her long legs, tight ass, sexy shoulders and thick, straight hair.

"Brick and leather," she muses. "Concrete floors."

She walks over to the one wall that isn't brick. The wall that used to be just plain white plaster but as time went by has been taken over by my busy hand. She reaches out and runs her fingers over my shit; the paintings, the sketches, even the tags. It's like she's running her hands over me when she does it, and I actually need to focus on breathing right.

"You did these," she says, her fingers tracing a large portrait of a man and his kid, both with skull faces. It's not a question.

I come up behind her. She smells way too good to be in a locked room with me. "Every tat I create's got to go up on the wall first."

She turns around, her back brushing up against the wall. I think about easing off her, telling her to get in my chair and let's get this show on the road. Fuck, let's get this show over and done.

But do I move?

Hell, no.

"Every tat?" she asks. "Even mine?"

A piece of her hair's escaped its pack, and I reach out to rescue it. My fingers brush her cheek and she breaths in, all quick and affected.

"No," I say. "Not yours."

Her eyes, those nutty, amazing eyes that I always begged her to keep on mine when we kissed or fucked, or hell, just shared a gallon of flat-assed coke after school at my house, flashed with gloom.

"Well, it's amazing, Rush," she says in a soft voice. "What you've done here. You should be really proud of yourself."

What I should be is naked, her in my arms, my mouth going to work on all those pretty parts I know make her wild. But that's off limits unless I want to suffer for all eternity.

"Come on," I say instead, backing up, feeling the heat of her roll off my body and die away. "Let's get started."

Like a moron—like the guy who just wants that heat back again—I reach for her hand and lead her over to my chair. "So, how's it feeling? Any irritation?"

She shakes her head. "Not bad. Frankly, my curiosity is irritating me more."

I laugh softly. "Let's have a look." I gesture to the chair.

"Should I take off…" She touches the bottom of her tank.

"Yeah." I grind the words out. My jaw's getting as hard as my dick now.

I watch her when I should be setting up. She pulls the tank over her head to reveal a cream-colored bra, and I fucking stare like a middle schooler getting his first look at a girl's naked skin. She hasn't changed much. Long, lean limbs, but serious, deadly curves. Her ass and tits have always turned my brain to cheese, and my dick to stone, and I swear to god, it's no different tonight. I honestly don't know how I'm going to get through this tat without touching her.

She straddles my chair, her thighs flaring out. My mind starts ripping out images of all the ways I could use that chair to pleasure her. And it's not the first time I've gone there. More than a few nights over the years, staring at that empty chair, picturing her in it, picturing me on my knees…

I frown. Thinking, fantasizing…they say it's healthy. I say it's bullshit.

I come up behind her, my skin vibrating with the need to touch her. The bandage lies directly above her bra strap, but I like a clear workspace, so I unclasp her, then grin when she inhales sharply.

"Should I take it off?" she asks me, and her voice is so breathy my cock knocks against my zipper.

"Only if it makes you more comfortable," I say, peeling off the tape holding the bandage to her skin.

"Just trying to make things easier for you, that's all."

"Real thoughtful," I say tightly. And maybe a little asshole-esque.

She sighs. "Rush…"

My fingers are moving too slow pulling up the tape. "Yeah, baby?"

"You don't have be a total prick for me to get how much you hate me."

Christ, her skin's soft. And warm.

I'm so pissed off at myself and at her, and how her body's calling for me to round first and keep going, like a goddamn third base coach, that I pull off the rest of the tape a little too hard. She sucks air through her teeth, and I turn away and drop the bandage in the trash.

I wish hating on her *was* the reason why I'm being such a prick. And not because my hands are fucking aching to be on her again, to steal around her waist and grope the shit out of her.

I'm silent as I set up, get the works in order. I'm kind of out of my mind with the tat I'm putting on her, but it's too late now. It's going to be sick, and permanent, and she'll have me on her for life.

Maybe as payment for ruining mine once upon a time.

She has her bra off when I turn back, gloves on, tat machine in hand. My iron—that's what we call it, even though it's all about the needle, not getting the wrinkles out of your shirts and shit—is a total extension of me, was from the first day we met. And I can't wait to get Addison under it again. Especially looking like that.

Fuuuuck.

The slip of cream silk is hanging over the chair along with her shirt, like an invitation. My fucking mouth waters like I haven't eaten in days. Her back is just endless inches of smooth, tanned playground.

"How's it look?" she asks.

My jaw goes tight and I can only laugh at her question. It's just so damn on the nose. "Looks pretty good. Your skin takes ink really well. Pain too, seems like."

She relaxes forward, dropping her chin. "I'm surprised by that actually. But maybe I've developed tougher skin these past five years."

I know she's speaking metaphorically, but I have this irresistible urge to lean in and run my tongue up her spine to check and see if it's true.

I look over my colors again, make sure they're lined up the way I like them. "Your skin will be sore," I tell her. "I normally wouldn't do this the same day, but if you can handle the pain—"

"I can," she insists.

Damn, it's like having the old Addison back when she talks that way. As I drop my head and get to it, I wonder if that's a good thing or the worst thing ever.

She hisses as the needle touches down, and I don't bother to ask her if she's all right. I want her to feel pain. Especially the kind that doesn't come from my needle. The kind that lasts years and refuses to let go of your soul no matter how hard you try, no matter how many women you fuck.

I work in relative silence for awhile, the sound of the machine and her steady breathing my only company. I'm falling in love with the design I'm putting on her. Even with all the turn-ons followed by the hard-ons, it could end up being one of my best pieces.

"I was surprised when I heard you were doing this," she says after a solid fifteen minutes. "With all the early scholarships to art schools, I thought maybe you'd go in that direction."

“I did,” I say, shading my yellow. “After skipping town, I checked out one in New York. Stayed there about six months before I picked up an iron and fell in lust.”

“In lust?” she says, a smile in her voice. “Not in love?”

“No. Never in love.”

She senses the bitterness in my tone and goes in for the kill. “Not with anything?”

“No.”

“Or anyone?”

I drop back, pull the needle from her skin. “What are you doing? You trying to find out if I’ve fallen for anyone since you? If I’ve fucked anyone since you?”

She stiffens. “Jesus, why are you so harsh? It’s like trying to talk to sandpaper.”

"I've always been that way, Addison. It's why we got together in the first place, *and* why you dumped my sorry ass. It's why you lied to me and went out with that buttoned up scoop of vanilla. And with what I saw you wearing today, you're still with him."

She's quiet for a minute or two, and even though I'm glad I said it, got it out after all these years, I still feel like a dick.

"What's rolling around in there?" I ask her. "What are you thinking?"

"I'm remembering when we first met. I think I was twelve."

I get back in the game. "Sounds about right."

"It wasn't the first time I'd seen someone smoking," she says, a grin in her voice. "But it was the first time I'd seen a kid doing it."

I sniff. "You walked right up to me and took it out of my hands. I thought you were going to stamp it out on the sidewalk. Color me stunned when you slipped it between your lips and took a drag."

She laughs softly. "I thought I was such a badass."

"You were, Ads." Fucking hell. *You were*.

She tightens up again. I do too. It's the first time I've used her nick in five years, and it's kind of like a knee to the balls. *Oh, shit*. Why are we doing this? Why am I? I could've heard what she had to say today at the convention center, finished the tat and been done with the whole thing.

But it was like once I had her in front of me, in my chair, in my eyeline, I couldn't let her go. Not this time. Not when I could do something to stop her.

"I don't think I was a badass, Rush," she says on a sigh. "A badass would've told the truth. A badass wouldn't have met up with someone behind her boyfriend's back. It's just that, being tossed around from house to house, eating one meal a day if that, no one wanting my ass…"

I wanted your ass, I almost say. But that would be suicide.

"I couldn't stay in that life."

My gut does that eating itself dance again. "And I was that life."

"I thought so."

"And vanilla ice cream was what? Happily ever after? China dishes and six bathrooms?"

"He was nothing."

"Bullshit, Ads. Don't do that. Not now."

She breathes, in and out, for a few seconds. "Okay. When he called that day and asked me to the dance—me, the other-side-of-the-boulevard girl—I felt—"

"Special," I interrupt.

"No. Saved."

Just that word—that one goddamn word—kills me. My jaw tight, I start running color over sections of black. I know this has got to hurt her, but I'm hoping the pain forces her to stop talking.

It doesn't.

"Rush, you came from the same thing," she says. "You were trying to keep your head above water just like me."

"Yeah, but I didn't think about swimming away from you to get it."

She releases a breath. “No, you didn’t. That’s why I’m here. That’s why I went to your house the very next day, why I called and wrote and tried to make appointments for the next freaking five years. That’s why I can’t seem to find joy in anything. Why I’m just…lost.”

My entire body goes rigid. My eyes narrow on the piece I’m inking into her skin.

“I’m sorry,” she says. “You have no idea how sorry I am for that night.” She’s quiet for a moment, then drops a bomb. “I loved you so much.”

My hand tightens around the iron. “I don’t want to hear any more.”

Then bomb number two. “I never stopped, Rush.”

“Goddammit, Addison,” I practically growl. “No more. I’m trying not to fucking scar you.”

"Then don't try."

I'm concentrating so hard my head hurts.

"Maybe the scar will do the trick," she says softly.

"What trick?" I grind out. "Be a constant reminder of your betrayal? Shit…that's what the tat is for."

"No." She laughs softly. "This tat is you. You on me always."

Inside my chest, my heart is slamming like a rock against my ribs, and down south, I've been hard for a solid thirty minutes. And as I near the finish line with her first ink, her virgin ink, I know this is just the beginning of me on her skin tonight.

Addison

I've been playing a game with myself for the past forty minutes. It's called Name That Tat. And I pretty much suck at it. With my eyes closed, and my brain turned to the *on* position, I once again try to envision what Rush is doing back there, what piece of art he's creating. I no longer think it's something mean, gross or insulting. In fact, after seeing what he's capable of on the wall to my right, I'm certain it's going to be jaw-dropping. But I do think it has the shape of a star about it. And I've tried in vain to follow his line work as the side of his hand brushes against my untouched skin, and his warm breath blows rhythmically on my inked skin.

It's not easy, though. As time ticks by, I feel this strange pain/pleasure sensation that makes me incredibly antsy and oddly turned on. I wonder if this is normal, or if it's all about Rush being behind me, seeing him after so long, after years of wondering and fantasizing. Just being this close to him makes my toes point inside my shoes, my breasts feel heavy, and my sex clench with a need so powerful that by the time he lifts the needle from my skin, my underwear is soaked.

I haven't been a pining nun in these past five years. I'm no sexual martyr. I've dated and had some good sex, and hoped that in time my need for Rush would dissipate. But it never did. Not for one moment. I don't know if it's because I lied to him and hurt him. I don't know if my guilt rules my obsessive desire, but as his fingers move over my irritated skin, massaging in that healing ointment with such slow, sensual care, my insides flare with heat. Despite the pain between my shoulder blades, every muscle in my body is poised and ready, every inch of skin, every hair follicle, every wet fold inside my pussy waits for its turn to be touched, to be tended to.

But will he? Does he even want to?

"All done," he says, placing what feels like plastic wrap over my skin.

I don't move. Not yet. "What do you think?"

"I think it's beautiful." His voice is dark, raw, pained. "I think the whole fucking thing is beautiful."

"Then what's wrong?" I ask, though I think I know. I hope I know. I hope he's feeling what I'm feeling and is just highly pissed off about it.

He doesn't say anything. Not right away. But I feel him, his nose, down near the left side of my waist. His breath brushes over my skin as he nuzzles me so damn gently I moan. My belly is clenching and my breasts are swelling against the leather chair, waiting, anticipating. *Touch me*, I silently beg. *Wrap your arms around me and fill your palms with my aching tits. God, you used to love my tits.*

I feel his mouth, his lips drag across my ribs. They're so soft and hungry. His tongue flickers out to taste me, dipping into the space between each bone. I gasp softly, my hands curling around the edge of the leather seat. My mouth is dry and hanging open as he moves higher, kissing each rib until he's right beneath my arm. His hair tickles my skin. My nipples bead, and my pussy is so wet now

I wouldn't be surprised if I'm soaking the chair I straddle.

And then he's gone. His warmth, his skin, his mouth, his tongue. And I sit there, my brain screaming for his hands, his nose, his lips, to please come back, come back and touch me again before I die, before I explode. Before I come right here on this chair where you've punished me for an hour and half.

"You can get up now, Addison," he says. "There's no more pain tonight."

His words slice through me, make me a little dizzy, make me think and worry. But I push off the chair and stand. It's only when I turn around to face him that I remember I'm not wearing a bra. His eyes catch on my chest and hold, and I can see now that I'm not the only one who's affected here. Still seated, Rush looks tense. His muscles and the veins in his neck are bulging. And his face, his expression…I swear I could come from that alone.

His jaw hard, his lips forming a thin, stressed line, his green eyes flaring with hunger, he reaches out and grabs my hips and pulls me to him.

"You want to see it, don't you, Addison?" he says, his eyes dragging up to meet mine.

At first I'm not sure what he means. It's difficult to think when your heart is beating so fast and hard against your ribs. The same ribs he nuzzled and licked a second ago.

"The ink," he says to me. "You want to see it?"

"You know I do," I return, my agitated breathing making my breasts rise and fall noticeably. "Can I look?"

He shakes his head at me.

My brows drift together. “I don’t understand.” My voice sounds as breathless and on edge as I feel. “You said when you were done—”

He yanks me even closer. “I’m not done. Are you?”

I stare down at him. His chin, his mouth, are dangerously close to my zipper. “No.”

His eyes bore a hole into mine. “Two hours, Ads.”

I’m shaking now. I know he can feel it. I know he can feel his effect on me. “For what?”

“Until the bandage needs to come off.”

“Oh.”

“Two hours.” He lifts one eyebrow. “There’s so many things I can do in two hours.”

My tongue darts out to wet my dry lips. He tracks it with his eyes.

“I could clean up here,” he says, conflicting emotions flashing in and out of his gaze. “I could take you back to wherever you’re staying, get you packing and on your way home.”

My chest seizes.

“Or I could get your jeans around your ankles and fuck your soaking wet pussy with my tongue.”

His raw words rip through me, stealing my breath. My knees feel weak, my blood is rushing crazy fast through my veins, and the wet heat he just mentioned fucking is snaking down my inner thigh.

His eyes pinned to mine, he nods. “I can smell you, Ads. Shit, the scent of your juicy slit’s been inside my nostrils for the past hour.”

“Rush, please,” I beg, only I have no idea what I’m begging for.

"So, what should I do?" His hands, one tanned, one covered in ink, drift from my waist inward, and his fingers play with the button at the top of my jeans. "I know what I want to do."

"Tell me." Please tell me. I need to hear it so badly.

Even though his eyes remain locked to mine, he flicks off the button and slides down the zipper. "I want to taste you one last time. Suck your pink clit into my mouth one last time before you walk away again."

My throat goes tight. I hate that he says that. I hate that he uses it right now, when I'm so fucking hot and desperate I won't say a word back. Because I didn't walk away. Yes, I broke things between us in a shitty, unforgivable way. But it was him, it was

Rush, who left. The very next day after the dance that ended it all. Quit school and disappeared.

His gaze is straight ahead now. He's pulling my jeans down, over my hips, and taking my drenched panties along with them. His nostrils flare and he sucks air through his teeth with every inch of skin he reveals. "Reach back," he says, sending my jeans to the floor. "Hold on to the chair."

I glance over to the door. "Rush. What about—"

"It's locked."

"You knew," I say, coming undone before he even touches me. There's just been too much need inside me, too much anticipation. "What might happen?"

His lust-filled eyes rise to mine. "It's you and me, Ads," he whispers against me, his breath fanning my wet, sensitive pussy. "We were combustible from the start."

As his hands rake up my torso, his tongue lashes at the outside of my sex. I gasp and squeeze the leather chair.

"Oh, fuck, baby," he says, squeezing my breasts in his large hands, rubbing his forehead along the top of my pelvis. "Nothing I loved more than going down on you."

He licks all the way through my slit. From the entrance of my pussy to the swollen bud inside my folds. And as he circles and flicks and laps at me, he moans and rolls my nipples between his fingers.

I glance down, breathing fast, and watch him suck me, his gorgeous, full lips glistening with my juices. He's so sexy, all that muscle and all that ink pressed up against me. I want him. All of him. Him inside me, him behind me, on top of me. So deep he can't get out, ever, not until he forgives me.

I'm so swollen now, so open and ready and desperate to come. I writhe and buck against his mouth. I feel insane and happy, and like I'll break apart. But I'm not ready to give in to what's surging through me yet, what's beckoning me closer. To the edge. To mind-blowing perfection. Because…what had he said? *One last time*? If I come, it's over. We're over. For good. I've said what I came here to say, told him the truth, told him what a stupid, scared fool I was, even told him my feelings for him haven't changed.

His hands leave my breasts and slip down underneath his chin. He presses his thumbs into my flesh and spreads my pussy lips apart. Wide. So wide I jerk and cry out.

And then his lips cover my clit and he suckles me. Over and over, drawing my distended flesh into his mouth.

A low, pained, groan escapes my throat, and I know I'm done for. Crying out, grinding myself against him, I explode. Flashes of light hit the backs of my eyelids as I shake and buck against his mouth, coming, creaming, feeling desperate for something, someone—RUSH—to fill me even as I linger in the shocking delights of release. I feel tears at the back of my throat. Long held tears that I have always refused to shed. And I push them back. I don't want him to see me cry, see me utterly wrecked.

Utterly vulnerable.

Not when he's going to send me home.

Still gripping the chair so hard I'm sure my nails have left a mark, I watch, breathing hard as Rush drags slow, wet kisses all the way up my belly, my ribs, suckling at the tip of each breast before lifting his head and facing me.

His gaze bears down on me. Those incredible green eyes eating me up like he just ate my pussy. He looks lethal and beyond sexy. "Where's your friend?" he asks me, though it comes out as more of a growl.

"Hotel," I mutter.

I'm dying—DYING—to reach out and yank down his zipper like he yanked down mine, but when I do, when I try, he stops me. He puts a hand over mine and steps away.

Just that small rejection makes my insides bleed. He can touch me, pleasure me, make me come, but he doesn't want my hands anywhere near him.

He reaches for my tank top, hands it to me. "Put this on. No bra."

My hands are shaking from my orgasm and from my anger, but I do as he asks.

When the tank is over my head, he moves back into my airspace and cups one of my breasts through the thin fabric. Instantly, my back arches and I lean into his touch. As he runs his thumb over the hard tip, I tell myself I have no shame.

His nostrils flare and he looks at me with hooded eyes. "Do you want to go back to your friend, Addison?"

"No," I say without a moment's hesitation.

He grabs my bra and shoves it in his back pocket. “Good answer.”

She's fucking unraveled me again. Screwed with my head again. Made me not only want her ass more than I've ever wanted it, but made me believe that maybe—shit, just maybe—there's a possibility for…something. Clearly, I'm mentally fucked, because instead of putting her on the back of my bike and dropping her wherever she and her friend are hanging their hats, I put her on the back of my bike and set a course for home.

She's wearing my helmet, and her arms are wrapped so tightly around my torso I sort of can't breathe. But I don't give a shit. The moon is full, stars are blinking hard and bright, we're alone on the desert road, and I just can't get there fast enough. Get my mouth on hers fast enough. Get my tongue back inside her fast enough. It's a real fatal flaw with me.

My mom knew it. Knew I had no business slowing down. She named me Rush because of how I was born. I was her first baby, and I guess they say that first babies take forever. Not me. Twenty minutes from home to hospital to in her arms. And from that day on, it's how I've lived my life.

As I take a tight curve, Addison squeals behind me and clings to my back like a terrified monkey. I could slow down, if I was a nice guy. Or shit, I could pull over to the side of the road, let her breathe for a second. But that might bring about some trouble. I'd probably be inclined to turn around and have her straddle me, wrap her legs around me as I drop her zipper again. And mine.

Shit, we don't need to get all the way naked. Not for me to slip inside. I know how wet she gets. I can still taste it.

I narrow my eyes and kick the chopper into high gear. I must be a fucking lunatic to be doing this. Or a masochist. Or shit, maybe both. But it's been a dream of mine to have her at my place. Have her see it, walk around inside it. Without ever knowing that she was who I thought about when I designed it.

I pull off the main road onto a dirt one that stretches up a ways and meets with my actual driveway. I bought this piece of land on the second anniversary of Wicked Ink. We'd been doing really well, and I'd been dying for something all my own, deep in the desert. It took a good year to build the contemporary stone, metal and glass structure, but it was worth the wait.

I kill the engine under the steel carport, then wait for Addison to slip off before following her. She already has my helmet off by the time I face her, and it's like holding back a bull when I see her bright eyes, flushed cheeks and sexy, just-fucked hair.

But her eyes aren't on me, they're combing the exterior of my house.

"Oh, Rush," she breathes, sounding so entranced I feel a fucking kick in my heart muscle. "You designed this. I can tell."

I don't say a word. I think my throat's not working right. Or maybe it's my lungs. I just take her hand and lead her inside the house. My gut is doing the knot dance again because as she stares at all the glass and metal, brick and stone, I wonder if she likes it or is overwhelmed by it. The place is pretty modern, maybe even cold to some.

Standing in the center of the living room, staring out the wall of glass doors leading to the view of the Red Rocks in the distance, she turns to look at me. “It’s beautiful.”

The knot inside me unravels instantly and I find myself grinning like an asshole. I take her around, show her every inch of my digs, preen like a douche every time she oohs and aahs over my shit. God damn, I don’t want to be this guy, this guy who feels giddy-ass relief that his girl approves of his pad. Because A: I shouldn’t give a shit. And B: She’s not my girl anymore.

We end up in the kitchen and I remember she’s a guest and not a permanent resident who knows her way around and has equal control over the fridge and its contents.

"You want something to drink?" I ask, grabbing the handle and pulling the stainless door open to see what I got.

"Sure." Addison leans against the counter all casual. She looks good in here, like she already belongs or something.

My hand tightens around the handle. "Nothing with alcohol for you."

"Hey, hey," she says on a laugh. The sound echoes through my house. I wonder idiotically if it'll stick around, maybe cling to the walls after she leaves.

"I'm over twenty-one, man," she continues. "Granted, it's just one year over. But that's legal."

“Alcohol can do funny things.”

“No doubt. Some of the shit I’ve see at school…”

“I’m talking about tats.” I stare into the fridge, not seeing a damn thing, my skin going tight around my muscles. “Don’t want the area to start bleeding. It’s not likely, but I’m not taking any chances.”

“Aww, you’re such a caring guy.”

I close the fridge with just a little too much force and turn to face her. “No. I’m not.”

Her brows shoot together and she pushes away from the counter. Her happy face, and that sexy but casual body language—both of which I seriously want to bottle and keep in my upstairs safe—go rigid.

"Okay, what just happened?" she asks, shaking her head at me, her eyes confused. "We were chilling. Had a back and forth that was easy and light, and…" She shrugs. "You turn dark again. What's going on, Rush? Did you bring me here to fight?"

My body flares up and my dick knocks at my zipper. Why did I bring her here? Was it because after tasting her back at the office, I needed more? I needed all of her? Or was it something besides that?

As I try to work out what I'm feeling, what I'm doing, my freaking intentions, my jaw goes so goddamn tight I'm worried about something snapping in there.

She takes a step toward me. "Rush…"

I back up like she's made of fire. "Don't want to fight."

"Okay, good." She nods. "Then what's up?"

"What's up?" I repeat, sounding a little manic. "Jesus…I'm such a fucking idiot."

"Why?"

My eyes lock with hers. I'm going off the rails. I can feel it. Why did she have to do this? Come back here and start shit up again? Make me want her? Make me remember how I've never stopped.

"Will you talk to me, please?" she says.

"I brought you here because I wanted to show you…" Fuck! I start, but can't finish. Because I'm a pussy. Because her eyes are trying to burrow into my chest and take a look at my heart.

"Show me what?" she pushes.

I turn away, walk away, head for the doors and for the Red Rocks beyond. I contemplate smashing the glass to bits, even though I can just open the fucking thing if I want out. It's just…I don't want her to peer inside of me. I don't want her to see that once-wrecked muscle because she'll see that it's no longer wrecked. That it's starting to look right and maybe open up a little.

"Rush," she calls, coming up behind me.

"Not now, Addison," I say, feeling nuts and out of breath. "Give me a sec."

"God, you're killing me here."

"Good!"

"What?"

I round on her, my anger, fear and lust colliding. "I said *good*! Fuck you, Ads. Good!"

Tears prick her eyes. She stares at me for one second, then turns around and heads to the kitchen counter and the small purse she'd dropped there earlier.

I'd fucking loved seeing her shit on my counter.

"What are you doing?" I ask, though it comes out harsh and demanding.

"I need to call a cab."

My heart sinks into my gut like it's made of steel and I hightail it over to her. "No."

Ignoring me, she digs in her purse and pulls out her cell.

I take it from her. "You're not going anywhere. Goddammit, Addison, I didn't say that to hurt you."

She turns and glares at me. "Sure you did, and you had every right to. I deserve it. I know I do. I fucked up. I knew what I had—I knew!" Those tears start falling. "But I threw it away. I'll regret it for the rest of my life, Rush, but I was fucking seventeen years old. We're morons at seventeen.

We think everything we do is right—that nothing has a consequence.” She grabs my shirt, yanks me to her. Her eyes are wild and glistening and gorgeous. “I’m asking you, begging you to forgive me so I can move on with my life—”

I cover her hand with my own and snarl, “You’re not getting my forgiveness.”

“Why not?” she cries out.

“Because I don’t want you to move on with your life!”

I grab her face and cover her mouth with mine. Her mouth has always been a hot and soft spot for me, and the one place I always wanted, but tonight it’s my way back from misery. I need her. More than I needed my tongue on her earlier. More than I need food or booze or my iron in my hand. I need my body against her, my dick inside her, deep and wet, just one last time to get her out of my system. Or fuck, that's what I'm going to tell myself with every inch I push myself inside of her.

Christ, whatever it takes to separate feeling from fucking.

As she works my zipper, I grab for the edges of her tank, and ease it up, breaking our kiss for a sec to pull it over her head. Then I take her face in my hands again and devour her. She tastes hot, like the desert we're alone in, and I drive my tongue inside her mouth to let her know that she belongs to me. Right now, she belongs to me.

Her hands fumble with the waist of my jeans, but she manages to get my fly undone and my cock in her hands. I groan as she fists me, and kiss her deeper. She meets me every step of the way, sucking my tongue into her mouth, biting at my lower lip.

Like I said, her and me, we were always combustible.

Her breasts are pressed up against my chest, the diamond-hard tips making me crazy with lust. I hate that I can't have her every way at once. Hate that my mouth can't be everywhere at once. Shit, that would rule with this girl.

I drag my mouth away from hers with a curse. Which causes her to release my dick. The thing instantly cries over the loss, dripping pre-come on my abs. But I gotta get those jeans off of her, those soaking wet panties. Breathless, her eyes half-lidded and hot, she wiggles out of the tight denim and tosses them aside with her foot.

I grin. I can't fucking help it. She's just so kickass. So fun. So desperate, like me.

Completely naked now, I see how wet she is, how the sweet-as-sin juice I sucked from her earlier is running hot again, down her leg, tempting me. My mouth waters, and I contemplate laying her out on my dining table and having a late supper. But then she's on me, her thumbs tucked into the waistband of my jeans. She pulls Denim and his friend Boxer Brief down so hard I almost lose my balance. She looks up at me and laughs. I do too, then kick both things in the same direction as her clothes.

For one second, maybe two, I let my eyes roam over her, take in that sexy body that makes my eyes cross with lust. Oh, the artwork I would love to brand her with. Something with a lot of color on her thigh…maybe some black and gray under one of her breasts. Then my gaze jacks up, locks with those mismatched peepers and I'm done. Fucking done.

I reach for her, around her, and cup her ass. The second I lift her up, she wraps her legs around my waist and grinds her wet pussy against the base of my shaft.

I groan. "It's been a long time since I've been inside you," I say, my eyes tight with hers. "And yet I remember every inch. How you feel, how you smell, how tight your pussy squeezes my cock when we come together."

"Oh, god," she breathes, her eyelids getting heavy. "Rush, don't make me wait any longer."

We're face to face, breath to breath, and as I lean in and take her mouth again, I lift her sweet ass in the air and set her right down on my cock.

Addison

I feel stretched. Filled. Like I don't want to move, the pleasure of having Rush inside me is so great. I wrap my arms around his neck and kiss him, bite at his lower lip, play tongue war as his fingers press into my ass with every slow yet deep thrust. I've completely forgotten where I am, where we are. It's just empty space, air to breathe while we fuck each other like rabbits.

He groans against my mouth, holding us tight together as he grinds his hips into me, circling, then driving upward again. My breasts bounce with each thrust, and my pelvis is completely slick with moisture. It's running down both our thighs, and I love that. Just like I love hearing him move, the slap of him against me. It's so primal, so uninhibited. Neither one of us is trying to hide our need, our desperation for each other. It's obvious in every guttural thrust, every drop of pre-come inside of me, every suck of my tongue into his mouth.

I rake my hands down his neck to his shoulders. God, his skin is so hot, so hard with lean muscle. I wish I could feel the artwork beneath my fingers as he drives into me.

"Addison," he rasps against my hungry mouth. "Tell me…"

"What?" I mumble nearly incoherently. "Anything."

"Tell me why you came back? Why?"

I groan. He's so deep inside of me now my walls are contracting around him. Much more of this and I'm going to come. "You know why!" I cry out.

"For forgiveness?" His fingers brush over the seam of my ass.

I can only nod. My breath is stalled inside my lungs and my heart is slamming against my chest. Oh, god…is he? Is he going to touch me there?

"Damn, woman." He eases his fingers lower, drenches them with my cream, then returns to my ass. "It's done. Okay, Ads? It's over. You have it. No more of this bullshit."

Slowly, he enters me with one wet finger. "Oh, fuck, you're tight. Around my cock and around my finger."

I cry out. It's too much. Pressure and pleasure and memories. This was something only we shared. I loved it. I loved him.

He moves us. Somewhere. A wall, I think. He presses back against it and bears down on me, fucking me so hard I scream, all the while using his finger in slow, gentle strokes. The combination is my downfall. I cling to him, my eyes clenched tight. I'm shaking, convulsing, writhing, a wave of dizziness coming over me. And yet, I can't stop. I buck against him, moaning that I need more, I need all of him.

"Oh yeah, that's it, baby," he snarls close to my ear. "Your pussy's fisting me, milking me."

My nails dig into his shoulders as I feel him jerk and grow impossibly bigger inside of me. I gasp, shove my hips forward. I can't get close enough. His finger presses deeper into my rear and his thrusts go hard, fast and deep, hitting that spot in me that sends my flying. And I'm off, gone.

Shattered. Crying out my climax, my eyes flood with tears. Waves upon waves of intense heat lash over me as Rush continues to fuck me, using my orgasm to send him into his.

"Oh, Addison," he groans, thrusting fiercely into me, chasing his high. "My Ads."

I feel the hot rush of his come bathe my walls, and I grip him even tighter, hold him even closer as he eases his finger out of me and satisfies my last clenches of orgasm with four deep, yet slow thrusts into my sex. God, this is right. This is it. How it's supposed to be. Finally, he slows, drops his head back against the wall and wraps his arms around my waist, locking me in.

"Fuck, Ads," he breathes.

“I know,” I say, dragging my tear-stained face across his shoulder. “I know.”

Without another word, he pushes away from the wall and heads out of the kitchen. Sweat clings to us both as he carries me down the long hallway. I know where we’re going. I saw it on my tour. His bedroom. It’s big and modern and right now that’s all I can register or care about because when we enter, he goes straight for the bed and lays me down, oh-so gently, on my side. No lights are on, but the moon’s magnificent glow streams in through the massive floor-to-ceiling windows. The sheets feel cool and soft against my skin, but they’re nothing compared to the hot, hard body that tucks in behind me.

For a good five minutes, or maybe it's an hour, I don't know or care, we just lie together like sweaty spoons. I stare out the window to the landscape in the distance and let myself acknowledge the perfection in the moment. Coming to Las Vegas, I hadn't even dreamed I'd get to share this again with Rush.

I close my eyes and try to calm my breathing. Tomorrow I'm supposed to go back, to home and school. I have a paper due on Monday…

"What are you doing?" Rush whispers against my neck.

I shiver. "I don't know." *Thinking. Trying not to think.* "I could easily fall asleep."

He groans softly. "Shit, me too. But, baby, there's not going to be any sleeping tonight."

I feel his cock, hard and ready against the curve of my butt. My back arches automatically. "You want me to stay?"

He's quiet for a second, and I wish I had a super power that allowed me to hear the thoughts of others. Or maybe just one other.

"Addison," he says finally. "I have you in my bed. You're not going anywhere. Not tonight, not..."

He stops himself. And I panic. The last thing in the world I want is for this moment to go south, and if he starts overthinking, that's exactly where we're headed. Whatever happens tomorrow, happens. Tonight, we're going to kiss, and lick each other, and laugh, and fuck. That's it.

I roll to my belly and give him a seductive smile. "I'm very open to being your prisoner."

His eyes instantly darken. “How open?”

As he watches, a grin pulling at his mouth, I come up on all fours. “How’s this?”

He groans. He’s so gorgeous and so completely captivating, I could stare at him for days without a break. No food, no water. Just Rush.

“Damn, Ads,” he practically growls. “That sweet ass kills me.”

As he slips a hand beneath me and plays gently, erotically with my nipple, I close my eyes and sigh. It’s done. I’m done. Forever. I swear, to whoever is up there directing traffic, this guy owns me. My heart, my body, every cell.

My pussy stirs with heat, and I squirm, wanting him again. Just the thought of him entering me, inch by steely inch, makes hot shards of pleasure rip through my sex.

My eyes open. His hand is gone from my breast, and he's behind me now, his fingers working the tape from between my shoulder blades.

"What are you doing?" I say, glancing over my shoulder.

"Taking off the bandage." He's flush against me now, the thick shaft of his cock moving tantalizingly between my sensitive flesh as he works. "It's been two hours."

Two hours? I feel a pang of anxiety, like time is moving too fast. Tomorrow's coming too quickly. "How is it?"

He sucks air between his teeth and his eyes lift to mine. "Perfect."

"Can I see it?" I feel the hard, wet pressure of his cock against my opening.

His eyes still locked to mine, he shakes his head. “Not yet,” he says, sinking into me with a groan. “Not yet.”

The morning light out here near the Red Rocks is so different than just twenty minutes away in Vegas. It almost looks like it's made out of crystal. And the sky is so damn blue. As I come up on one elbow and take a gander out the window, I think this might be the most perfect morning I've ever seen.

Or maybe it's the exact same as every other morning, but I got this girl in my bed.

I sniff and shake my head. I slept maybe an hour last night. I had this crazy-ass urge to keep watch over her. You know, like some jerkoff roaming the desert was going to find his way up here and try to break in. Steal shit.

Steal my girl.

Whoa, whoa, whoa, dickhead, I tell myself. Don't do that. For your own fucking sanity, don't do it.

My eyes cut to her. She has her back to me, a sheet at her waist, and that light I was going on about a moment ago, it's hitting my tat so perfectly my fucking guts roll over.

What the hell am I going to do? One-night-onlys happen more often than they probably should for me, but one night bliss sessions with the former love of your fucking life? Addison came here for two reasons: to tell me the truth about why she dumped my ass for another guy in front of an entire puberty-infested gymnasium; and to apologize for it.

Done.

That memory used to kill me. She'd said she was sick that morning, didn't feel good enough to go to the dance. Sure I'd rented a tux and my stepdad was going to spend the night drinking so he'd offered me his car, but it wasn't like it was prom or anything. Just homecoming. And since neither of us played a sport or carried pom-poms, I didn't care. Thing was, I cared for *her*. I'd opened up a can of Campbell's, and brought it over to her house. The chick who answered the door was really forthcoming with the information, grinned when she said it and everything.

The Campbell's had gone into the bushes and I'd gone to the school. Ads and me, we never really tried to be friends with anybody else. We were so tight. I think that was the kick in the 'nads for me.

We were best friends, and there she was—so not sick—and slow dancing with that buttoned-up vanilla douche from the wrestling team.

Cops would've been called that night if Addison hadn't stepped in, told me to take a walk. Course, my walk was a lot farther than she or I expected.

Next day, I packed all my shit and took a bus to New York. Refused every goddamn attempt Addison made to contact me. Like Ads said, we're all morons at seventeen.

My eyes move over her skin. Everything's different now. Our lives, our futures. And yet, this thing between us hasn't died. If anything, it's gained in strength like a tornado or a tsunami. Vanilla was a test, a break in the weather. But now…what?

She said she still loves me, but she never said anything about a second chance. About us trying this again. For all I know, she's got someone back in Cali.

Once again, my guts plummet, rollercoaster-style. I never asked if she was seeing someone. Maybe I should've. Or maybe I should just go with the I-don't-give-a-flying-fuck attitude.

She moves then, stretching, arms up, back arching, butt lifting my way.

Blood surges, heavy and painful, into my cock and I drop onto my back, lock my hands behind my head. Granted, I'm a horny motherfucker, but I've never wanted a girl like I want Addison. It's always been like that. Even after I left town. I'm not proud to admit it, but I couldn't stop my mind from dropping her face and those eyes a few times when I was with someone else.

Thing is, back in the day, I'd known. I'd *known* we belonged together. Not just until grad, but for the long haul. We were just, as the old folks say, meant for each other. But like anything partnership-related, it takes two.

"Rush?"

She utters my name all sleepy and sexy and turns over, drapes herself across my chest and groin, snuggles in tight. My cock lifts against her thigh and instantly, she lowers her leg and wraps her hand around my shaft.

I forget everything, even my name—Joe? Darrell? Bob?—as she begins to stroke me off. At first it's just light, sensual petting, Easy Like Sunday Morning kinda thing, but as I pump into her hand, and as the head of my dick sports a few drops of come, she tightens her hold.

Her head is tucked into my neck, and as she works me over, she bites and laps at my skin.

"Tongue tracers," she whispers, licking down my neck and over my collarbone as she jacks me.

"What?" I manage to kick out.

"Your ink," she says, moving farther, running her tongue around my nipple.

Shit, if she's going to be using her mouth that way I need to get that thing pierced, like yesterday.

Speaking of using her mouth…I groan as her head snakes down over my belly and lands dead center. My cock is throbbing in anticipation. It loves her hand, needs her pussy. But right now, it wants her mouth.

She looks up at me, her lips resting on the head of my prick.

"Fuck, I hope you're thirsty, baby."

"Parched beyond reason, Rush." She grins, then sticks out her pretty pink tongue and licks into the slit.

I groan. "You remember how much I come?"

She nods, her eyes bright and excited, like it's fucking Christmas morning.

I thrust gently toward her. "Every drop then, Addison."

Her nipples bead as she nods again. Then her head drops and she sucks me deep, taking me all the way to the back of her throat. I curse, loud and guttural, going momentarily blind. Shit, her mouth is hot and wet. Then she retreats, her lips just covering the head now. Her eyes lift to mine and they shine with sexual power.

Go to it, baby, I want to say. *Take whatever you want, however you want it.* But my voice is lost. Gone on a voyage far, far away.

She pushes her lips all the way over the head now, slowly working her way to the root. And when she gets there—what does she do? Grab my fucking ball sack. Come beads at the tip of my dick and she licks it right up, moaning when there's nothing left.

As she gently massages my testicles, she works her tongue up and down my shaft, Popsicle-style, then drops her head and sucks me deep. I thread my fingers in her hair and start pumping into her mouth. That really gets her going. She moans and closes her eyes and rubs her gorgeous tits against my thigh. Breathing hard, my gut clenching, my gaze lands on her upper back, the artwork I put on her—my brand—and stays there.

I come hard, my balls pulling up, my dick swelling. I know it's a river I'm pumping into her, but she drinks me down like I'm the best goddamn thing she's ever tasted.

And maybe I am. Because to me, she's the best I've ever had. The only thing I want.

As I keep thrusting, slower and slower, she eases back and starts licking me clean, tending to me all sweet and shit. After going all night, I swear to god I should be soft and done, but it's Addison. She's my candy, my addiction. My dick stays hard for her. It knows her. It wants her. Again and again.

I reach down and grab her under the shoulder blades. I lift her up, then slowly, inch by inch, place her down on my shaft. Her honey walls instantly curl around me, cream around me.

I watch her as she rides me, as her fingers dig into my chest—as her goddamn eyes cling to mine. Right now, I'm not clear. Right now, my heart is having trouble knowing the difference between sex and love. And that's got to be because with Addison there is no difference.

When she starts to really pick up speed and my hands grope at her perfect ass, I close my eyes and swallow the words that are fighting to get out of my mouth.

I love you too, Ads.

Never stopped.

Her walls clench around me.

Never want to stop.

Addison

Lisa: WTF, Addy! Where are u?

Me: W/rush. What's wrong?

Lisa: I've been trying 2 reach you!

Me: Sry! Phone off.

Lisa: It's OK. Just worried abt u.

Me: I'm fine. Sore & fine:)

Lisa: Gross.

Me: Heh heh.

Lisa: When I didn't hear from u I got freaked, went 2 that tattoo parlor.

Me: ?!?!?

Lisa: I tried 2 find out where rush lives, but that asshole vincent wouldn't give it up.

Me: Oh, hon, I'm sorry. I told u I'd prob B out all night.

Lisa: He was a real dick 2 me. Said some things...

Me: What did he say?

Lisa: When r u coming bk 2 the hotel? I really need 2 talk 2 u.

Me: WTF did he say, Lis???

Lisa: Just come, ok?

Me: K. I'll b there in 1 hr.

I look up. Rush is staring at me, all gorgeous and heavy-lidded and tousled hair, and wearing only his ink and a pair of black sweats that hang appetizingly on his hips. We're sitting on top of his sleek wood table outside on his massive deck. The sun is shining and a killer breeze is rolling off the desert. There's a bunch of food laid out between us: bagels and cream cheese and fruit. And right before I got Lisa's text, Rush was mentioning something about spreading that cream cheese on my stomach instead of his bagel.

I inhale deeply. I wish—really, really wish—I could pretend I didn't pick up my phone to check messages, stay in Rush & Addy Land all day. But my friend needs me, and we're supposed be driving back to L.A. in a few hours.

Rush lifts one eyebrow at me and my skin heats up instantly. The guy's just walking, talking, breathing sex.

"Your friend okay?" he asks.

I pick a grape from the bunch and roll it between my fingers. "I don't know. Something's wrong. She went to Wicked Ink last night."

"Why?" His brows draw together.

Jesus, even a confused frown on him is hot. Everything he does, every look, every word, I just melt. How the hell am I going to leave here, leave him, and go back to my life?

My vanilla life.

"She's worried about me," I say.

"She think I abducted you?"

His green eyes flash with equal parts heat and amusement. I die. Or sigh. Or both.

"Something like that." I pop the grape in my mouth, and when the juice bursts inside me, all I can think about is us, Rush and me and what we have together. What's happened between us in the past twenty-four hours. How we've fallen back into it, into each other. And it's like no time has passed. We joke and touch and tease so damn easy.

But does he see it? Or was this a kickass twenty-four hour reunion/sex marathon, and it's over now, and we both go back to our lives? Because he hasn't said anything. Not one word about me leaving or not wanting me to leave.

"She had a run-in with Vincent," I say. "Trying to get your address out of him."

He teases a couple of grapes from their stem. The thing relents way easily. *I know the feeling, my purple friend.*

"I'm guessing that didn't go over well. Everyone at Wicked knows not to give out my personal information."

"Is he a bad guy, Vincent?" I ask.

Rush shakes his head. "No. Just a horny guy."

"Like you?" I smile.

He snorts. "Oh, baby, that dude is way worse than me. I'm into one woman beneath me, on top of me, on her hands and knees in front of me."

Every cell in my body reacts to the words, and the suggestive look he gives me while saying it. *Cream freaking cheese*, I want to cry out. *What were you going to do with the cream cheese, dammit?!?*

But Lisa's my friend, my bestie, my beeyotch, and I will always have her back. Especially when she needs me.

"He wouldn't act stupid, would he?" I ask. "Force something?"

"Hell, no." Rush gives me a serious look. "The guy's a total slut, for sure, but he's not a pusher." He pops the grapes in his mouth one by one, and I've never felt so jealous of fruit in my life. "I don't know what went down, but if she went nuts wanting my address, he might've told her to take a hike in bright colors, if you know what I'm saying."

I do. And Lisa, though fun and outgoing, a real free-spirit, has a hard time with conflict. She's never told me everything about her home life, but from what I gathered her parents were going at each other 24/7.

My eyes travel over the tattoos on Rush's arms and chest. Just the thought of not being able to touch him again makes me sick to my stomach.

My eyes lift to meet his. "She needs me," I tell him. "And I've got school in the morning. And a paper due." I laugh, but it comes out as more of a choke. "Haven't even started it."

His eyes instantly lose their light, and my heart starts bleeding. "Okay."

"Give me a ride?"

"Course. But first…" He drops down from the table, then helps me.

Before I can say a word, he takes my hands and leads me inside the house. I wonder what he's up to, hope stupidly that it involves his arms around me and his lips crushing against mine, but then he leads me into the bathroom and in front of the mirror.

He looks at me, brows raised. "Ready?"

His art. On me.

I can't believe I've gone all morning without thinking about it. Remembering it. I'm suddenly nervous, clammy. Damn, I've been wanting to see the design Rush inked into me so badly, but now…I don't know. I'm scared of what it is and what it means. Or worse, doesn't mean. Maybe it's some thickly-lined tribal marking or a Hawaiian pin-up girl.

I'm wearing one of Rush's shirts, black and button down, and hits mid-thigh. And as I stand there in the middle of his gorgeous white and gray bathroom, I work buttons off with trembling hands for the second time in twenty-four hours.

After I'm done, I let him draw it off me. Wearing only a pair of his boxers, my nerves battering me, I look away from his hot, hungry eyes and glance over my shoulder. The moment my eyes connect with the stunning blast of color and form between my shoulder blades, I gasp, then cover my mouth with my hand. Eyes wide, I move around, seeing the piece from all different angles.

I turn to face him, slightly stunned by his choice. "It's a compass."

He nods, his leaf-green eyes a little wary.

I chew my lower lip. My heart is so close to the edge I'm almost afraid to ask. But I have to. Especially now, with all that's happened between us. "To find my way back home?"

His eyes close and he inhales deep. When he opens them again, he looks calmer, more in control—more like Rush. He shrugs. "You said you were lost, Ads. This'll help you find your way."

Not to me. Not find your way back to me.

Pain sears my insides, grief too, but I'm not going to let him know it. Nothing was promised here. It was only forgiven, and isn't that why I came? Isn't that what I really want?

The lie in that forced belief protects me, keeps me from bursting into tears, flinging myself into his arms and begging to stay. Or shit, begging him to ask me to stay. Because in truth, what I really want is him.

My eyes lift to his, but they don't stay long. "I should get dressed. Get back to the hotel. To my friend."

To reality.

I take the long way to her hotel. I know it's a completely fucked up way of keeping her close to me for as long as possible, but I don't give a shit. Everything inside of me is raging at the idea of letting her go. And the outside's not far behind. My skin is hardcore addicted to her. Like even now, with her arms wrapped around my waist, it's just not fucking tight enough.

Jesus.

As we hit the Strip, I take my turns easy instead of how I like them, fast and as close to upside down as possible without getting my skin peeled off by the asphalt. Because we're close. Too close. I don't know what we're doing here, what I'm doing, but I don't want to push her. If I push her and she fucking kicks me to the curb again, I'm done for. As in, major therapy and lots of colorful pills.

When we pull into the hotel's driveway, I don't stop in front of the sliding glass doors. Those bozos who check bags and shuttle tourists around aren't going to witness our farewells. Shit, I don't want anyone to see it, especially me. Instead I park down a ways, in the shadows of the building.

I step off the bike, then help her. I think my hands are shaking, which they've never done—ever. But this girl, she just fucking tears me up. I watch as she pulls off my helmet and holds it out to me. Her long hair is mussed, her cheeks are pale, and those eyes—fuck me—those mismatched eyes that belong to me, well, at least the one, bore into mine. And this time, I let her. I let her look. I let her take a good, long gander inside my ribs to my newly repaired and fully-functioning heart.

What do you see, Ads? I want to ask her. Grab her by the shoulders and force her to tell me. Tell me she wants nothing else but me. But shit, that's not fair. Twenty-four hours can't demolish a whole life. She has friends and school. Shit, she's graduating in a few weeks.

"Addison…"

Her eyes prick with tears and she shakes her head. Really fast, really manic. Her hands are balled into fists and she looks like she's about to lose it. And frankly I'm not far behind.

"Call me?" she rasps out.

"Sure," I return, my gut rolling, eating itself alive because I don't know if I can. I don't know if I can hear her voice and not go insane. Wouldn't it better to block her ass out, leave it here on the stained Vegas concrete and go back to real life?

She starts to walk away, but I grab her wrist and haul her back against me. She melts into me like chocolate, and I breathe in the scent of her hair. For several moments, we cling together like scared monkeys, then I release her. Our eyes connect one last time before I turn away and straddle my bike. I don't look up as I drop my brain bucket on my head and kick start the engine. Don't look back as I haul ass away from the curb.

Addison

"You sure about this?"

Lisa's sitting in the passenger side of my car with the door open, grilling me for the millionth time. She's super wary now. Of Rush, of anyone who works in that Den of Sin, as she calls it. She refuses to give me exact details of what went down when she went there last night, but I get the feeling it's not what I thought it was. Not Vincent hitting on her hard. She did say he was a giant asshole, and had insulted her. But the thing that concerned me most was the look on her face when she said it. Like she was questioning herself, unsure of herself. And that so isn't Lisa.

"I'm positive," I tell her. "See you in a few days?"

She nods and gets out of the car, tosses her bag over her shoulder. I bought her a plane ticket home, back to L.A. because I'm going to need my car.

She shuts the door, but sticks her head through the open window. "Call me tonight."

"I will. Promise."

"Even if you're happily being held against your will."

"Swears." I grin.

"You're not missing graduation."

"Oh, come on," I say, all serious now. "Never. I'll be there. You and me, side by side in our ugly gold gowns."

She snorts. “Seriously, why did they have to choose that color?”

“Right?” I say, laughing.

She looks at me and shrugs reluctantly. “Tell Rush I said hi, okay? Then tell Vincent I said he’s an asshole, and doesn’t know anything about anything.”

I drop my chin and say pointedly, “You’re going to tell me what was said there at some point, right?”

She smiles softly and readjusts her bag. “Love you, Addy.”

“Bye, Beeyotch,” I say affectionately.

“Bye, Whore,” she returns, then blows me a kiss before she heads into the terminal.

The second she's gone, my heart starts pounding away, bass drum-style. I pull away from the curb, and set my course for the coming sunset and the Red Rocks. I don't know what I'm walking into. I don't know what he'll say or do, but I just don't care at this point. I love the guy. Like to the moon and beyond kind of love, and I'm going to tell him so. I'm going to tell him that we belong together. Good, bad, amazing, scary, shit to work out—we're destined.

It takes me a good thirty minutes to get to Wicked Ink, but when I pull into the parking lot and slip between a few motorcycles and a Mercedes, my heart feels close to exploding. I know what I'm doing is the right thing, the only thing, but I'm scared. I know Rush still has feelings for me. I saw it in his eyes from the second he looked up at me in the convention center. But that doesn't mean he wants me back, wants anything more than what we had in the past twenty-four hours.

But I have to find out.

My entire body trembles as I walk through the front doors. Unlike last night, the place is littered with customers. The owners of the vehicles outside are seated and standing in the waiting area, and some of them glance my way as I head for the recep desk.

"Back again, beautiful?"

Standing behind the desk, checking out an appointment book, is Mr. Asshole himself, Vincent.

He's wearing black jeans and a distressed gray t-shirt with a picture of a snake coming out of a skull's mouth, the sleeves rolled up to his shoulders. He's tall and lean, both ears and one eyebrow pierced, and he's nearly completely tatted up. I'll admit it. The guy's intimidating, and gorgeous. Nothing compared to Rush, of course. But, then again, no one and nothing compares to Rush.

I shrug lightly. "I think I might be addicted."

He grins, wide and wicked. "That's how it is with ink. You can't have just one."

I lean on the counter. "Kind of like women?"

His black as night eyes widen. "Who you been talkin' to, little girl?"

I shrug casually, some of my nerves dissipating in the back and forth we have going here. "Heard you met my friend last night."

He nods. “Cute. A little uptight, but cute.”

I bristle at the assumption that my best friend is anything but 100% awesome. “She was worried about me. I think you were a jerkoff to her.”

“Nope. Just asked her out.”

That couldn’t be the whole story. “Well, she’s not your type.”

“Sweetness, if a girl’s got tits and a warm pussy, she’s my type.”

My mouth drops open.

He laughs. “You looking for Rush?”

“Yes.” Good god, this guy. Now I’ve got to know what went down. Tonight, I’m going to force it out of Lisa.

He points behind me with one of his tattooed fingers. “Right behind you, dollface.”

I whirl on the spot, and just like that I forget anyone else exists. I saw him only a few hours ago, but it's like I haven't seen him in years. Again. My gaze rakes over his face, swooning over it, memorizing it, in case this doesn't go well. He's wearing dark blue denim and a white tank top that shows off his tongue-tracing ink to perfection. I swallow the saliva that has quickly pooled in my mouth and force a smile. "Hey."

"Hey." He looks on edge, maybe confused as to why I'm there. Maybe disappointed that I'm there at all.

I chew my lip. My heart is slamming against my ribs so hard I think I'm bruised. I feel eyes on me, feel their judgment, too.

"You don't have an appointment, Ads," he says, his tone calm. Not cool. But calm. "And I'm pretty booked up."

Oh my god, what am I doing? He doesn't want this. Doesn't want me. And yet, I forge ahead because I refuse—REFUSE—to fucking have another regret where he's concerned. "This will just take a sec."

He nods, knocks his chin in the direction of his room. "Come on in—"

I never let him finish. I'm too keyed up, and this is it. My moment. To be accepted or to go down in flames.

"I love you," I burst out.

The entire room goes silent. Rush's face darkens. His eyes, too.

"Ads..."

"No," I continue, sounding nuts even to my own ears. God knows what I must look like. "No, that's not right. I'm fucking crazy about you!"

"Damn, brother," Vincent mutters behind us.

Rush turns and snarls at him, "Shut up." Then reaches for me. "Come on. Let's do this in private, Ads."

I draw back. "No." I shake my head at him. "Five years ago, I insulted you in front of a room full of people. Today, everyone's going to hear how fucking amazing you are."

He looks a little stunned, but I press on, my stomach churning. "I've always been crazy about you. You're it for me. Everything. My heart, my guts. My family, my best friend. You're the hottest lover in existence. And you make me feel special, like I matter, like I'm the only one in the world for you." I look at Vincent and flip him off. "That was for you, asshat."

Everyone hoots, and Vincent grabs his chest and groans, "Oh hot damn, I think I love her."

"No you don't," Rush snarls again. "And shut up."

I stare at him. Eyes locked. I don't care about anything else. "I want to do this, Rush. Me and you. Do you want to do this?"

"What about school, L.A., your paper?" His body, his sexy, inked-up body is so tense, so on edge. "Isn't that thing due tomorrow?"

I grin. I grin so wide it hurts. "I don't give a shit about my stupid paper. I'll get a fucking extension." I take a step toward him and stop. "I love you. Like crazy kind of love, understand me?"

He nods, real slow, his eyes so dark green they're nearly all iris. "Yeah, baby, I understand. I fucking love you, too. Crazy."

Tears scratch at my throat. I can't believe what I'm hearing. Can't believe we're doing this. Again. Starting over. Starting clean.

His lip curls and he growls at me. "Get your sweet ass over here."

I squeal and dive into his arms. He lifts me and grabs my backside, tucking me into him. Smiling like I just won the lottery—and let's face it, I fucking did! I wrap my legs around his waist and cross my ankles behind his back, locking him in tight.

"What now, Rush?" I whisper against his mouth as everyone hoots and catcalls around us. "What do we do now?"

He grins, wicked and sexy. "Let's start with an epic kiss, baby and see where we go from there."

The End

WICKED INK CHRONICLES

SHATTERED *ink*

NEW YORK TIMES BESTSELLING AUTHOR

LAURA WRIGHT

Addison

"You're kidding me with all this, right?" Lisa asks, her pointer finger tracing an imaginary Z down my body.

"All what?" I ask with slight irritation.

Lisa's crystal blue eyes, expertly rimmed in charcoal, narrow. "The toddler-napwear-meets-prison-inmate thing you're working."

The ocean breeze kicks my hair around my face. "Orange is the new black, Lis."

She looks insulted. "That's insane. Who said that?"

"I don't know. I think I heard it on Colbert last week."

"Colbert is a comedy show, Addy."

Tired, and not up for the night out my best friend has dragged me to once again, I take a step back, lift my arms. "Look, I see nothing wrong here. Just, you know, trying to be comfortable on a Thursday night."

"You look like you're headed to bed."

"I wish I was," I return with a bit of a pout, then silently amend, to *Rush's* bed. His big bed, cool sheets, and that hot, hot body I miss so much it hurts. I groan.

"You're losing it, Addy. You know that, right?"

I frown at her, but inside my mind I'm screaming YEAH, I DO.

Growing more exasperated with me by the minute, Lisa glances over her shoulder at the dozens of people coming in and out of the large Santa

Barbara oceanfront house, spotlighted in moonglow and about thirty iPhone screens. I can practically feel her urgency to get in there, mix it up, flirt her sexy leather ass off with all the boys she's been crushing on at school. But I'm keeping her from it. With my orange sweatpants and tear-stained t-shirt.

When she turns back, she looks mutinous. "I'm just going to say one thing to you: Vegas."

My insides go instantly hot and soft. It's a depressing feeling, but addicting and predictable. Kind of like my life has been over the past five weeks. When Rush and I chucked the past and decided to try this again, I was so happy. So excited. A second chance at a first love. But as Lisa put it, I'm losing it. In the past five weeks, I've only seen him three times, and for no more than a day or two. I have school and finals and graduation, and he has work and travel. It's like the most beautiful torture in the world, seeing him. I'm on a high when I'm around him. When he's gone, I crash. And I can't seem to bounce back. I'm utterly and completely addicted to him. I'm jealous of anything and anyone who gets to be near him, and there are actually times when I don't give a shit about graduating, about getting my marketing degree—about a job or a future. I just want to be in his atmosphere. I just want those eyes locked on mine, and those inked arms around me.

Of course, I haven't told him any of this. I don't want him to think I'm a loser. I don't want him to know the truth. I don't want him to walk away from me—or shit, run—because this time, it's not just love that would be lost. It'd be my heart, my breath…my sanity.

"Vegas, Addy," Lisa repeats, her perfectly arched brows lifting expectantly. "You owe me."

I sigh, at her, at myself and my crazy thoughts, and stuff my hands in the pockets of my orange sweatpants. "Come on, Lis. I paid you back for the convention a million times. Don't make me remind you—or myself—about that waxing party I helped you host."

Her mouth twitches. "No, sister friend. This isn't payback for the convention. This is for all the drives back and forth to the airport, the hours of listening to Rush's messages and trying to decode what he's *really* saying, the mornings I pull your ass out of bed and to class."

I actually recoil. "Seriously?"

"Hells yeah, seriously."

Some random guy walks by and gives Lisa a very dazzling, very appreciative smile. I don't blame him. She looks hella sexy in her tight leather pencil pants, low-cut lacy top and messy side braid. As she returns the smile, her expression curling into one of heat and promises, she waves at him. For second, I remember what it's like to flirt casually and just have a good time—act my age—and I don't miss it. Any of it. I only miss him.

I inhale deep and exhale heavy. God, this is bad. I shouldn't be this obsessed, this close to the edge, over a guy. I know Rush isn't feeling this way. Or at least he doesn't act like it. When we talk or see each other, he's chill, sexy, into me, for sure. But not like this—not like me.

When Lisa turns back to face me, takes in my relaxed-wear once again, she sighs. "Look. I know you miss him, Addy. I know you're head over heels, as the kids say. I know you want to be with him every second of the day. But you're starting to fall apart."

"Starting?" I say on a slightly manic laugh.

Lisa remains serious. "It's so not like you."

"I know." I shake my head. "I've never felt like this, Lis. Sometimes it's actually hard to breathe. It's more than just loving him, it's the fear of losing him. Just the thought of it breaks me apart inside. I don't know what to do with that."

Her expression softens. "I get it. I do. But you're going to have to hold back and chill out. What you're working here isn't cute, if you know what I mean. I believe the boys call it Psycho Bitch."

"Nice." But I know she's right.

"Maybe you need to take a little break from each other?"

"No." The word is out of my mouth fast and impassioned.

"Date other people?"

"Impossible."

Lisa's lips press together in a worried frown. For a second, she just stares at me. Then she shrugs. "Okay."

I know that word, *and* that look. She's freaked out by me. *Welcome to the club, sister friend.* "I'm sorry."

She shakes her head.

"No, seriously," I continue. "I'm sorry I'm such a mess. I'm sorry I'm being such a shit-tastic friend."

"Don't worry about it. I love my little train wreck in orange." A smile tugs at her lips.

I'm surprised when my mouth curves upward. "Okay. So, let's forget about my insanity and obsessive needs for a few hours. We're going to party. Hard. Loose. Wild."

She laughs. "Oh, Jesus."

"And." I gesture to my offending ensemble. "Just to show you I'm trying, I'll go home and change."

Lisa shakes her head. "No, you're fine. Actually, maybe it's better this way. Dolled up, you bring competition to the field, and you know I'm good with getting all the attention. Come on, beeyotch." She grabs my hand and leads me through and around several small pockets of students and up the path to the front door. "And for the record, fashion-wise, orange isn't the new anything. Except maybe a huge boner killer."

29160

Made in the USA
Lexington, KY
23 March 2015